Victor's Party

Andersen Young Readers' Library

Hazel Townson

Victor's Party

Illustrated by Tony Ross

Andersen Press · London

First published in 1990 by
Andersen Press Limited,
20 Vauxhall Bridge Road, London SW1

British Library Cataloguing in Publication Data
Townson, Hazel
  Victor's party.
  I. Title II. Ross, Tony, 1938 –
823'. 914 [J]
ISBN 0-86264-276-0

Typesetting by Spectrum Typesetting Ltd., London N1
Printed and bound in Great Britain by Courier International Ltd.,
Tiptree, Essex

Contents

*For Nicholas Flugge, always my
first young reader and valued critic*

1
Loner

'How come that boy's always sitting around on his own?' asked Victor Lovat's dad. 'Has he no friends, or what?'

Victor's mother smiled fondly.

'Our Victor likes his own company. I guess he's a bit of a loner.'

'Loner?' Arnold Lovat was aghast. No son of his had any right to be a loner. Lovats were popular people, right in the middle of things. Lovats were leaders of men. He began to wonder if he had been away too long. Perhaps he ought to give up the Merchant Navy and take a home-based job to keep an eye on things?

'Well, it's time he cultivated some friends. He can have a party.'

A party?

Victor raised a wary eye from his library book.

'It's five months to my birthday,' he said.

'Who's talking about birthdays? You don't have to grow older to have a party.'

'But you need a reason,' Mrs Lovat put in anxiously. 'You can't just throw a party like that, out of the blue. It's weeks and weeks to Christmas.'

She knew very well that Victor hated parties.

'You can do anything you like if you put

your mind to it,' retorted Mr Lovat. 'And there's no time like the present, whilst I'm home on leave. Get some invitation cards and start laying in supplies.'

He tossed a handful of fivers on to the table, but Mrs Lovat stared at them as if they were deadly snakes. As for Victor, his heart had picked up speed as he felt himself prised away from his comfortable fantasy world and obliged to dip a toe into the icy waters of real life.

'But Dad – !'

Arnold Lovat swept away all protests with a lordly gesture.

'A proper do, that's what we'll have. No less than twenty guests, girls as well as boys.'

'Twenty?' echoed Mrs Lovat. 'We haven't got twenty cups, for a start. And I don't know where you think they're all going to sit.'

Mr Lovat gave a great shout of disgust.

'Haven't you ever heard of paper cups? Haven't you ever sat on the floor? Honestly, anybody would think you'd been asked to put up the Royal Family for a fortnight.'

Victor, his face as colourless as tripe, flopped back into the depths of his armchair, weak with shock. Never mind the cups and chairs; where was he to raise twenty friends when at the moment he didn't possess a single one?

'And seeing that lad spends so much time in the library, he can look for a book of party games. We'll organise it properly, not leave anything to chance. In fact, this will be the

11

best party this town's ever been privileged to see. I might even be persuaded to play my accordion.'

Sighing, Mrs Lovat gathered up the money.

'Well – no more than twenty, then. Twenty's the absolute limit.'

She knew from long experience that it was no use arguing with her husband once he had

made up his mind. She felt sorry for Victor who, unlike his dad, would never be the life-and-soul of anything and craved only to be left in peace. She could foresee nothing but tears and trouble.

As for Victor, he felt as though he had just been condemned to death.

2
Orphans

'Want to come to a party on the twentieth?' Victor Lovat asked gloomily.

'Whose party?'

'Mine.'

'Yours?' Becky Ward could not hide her amazement, for Victor Lovat never had parties. 'It's not your birthday, is it?'

'No.'

'What you having a party for, then?'

Victor shrugged uncomfortably.

'He's getting engaged,' giggled Alison Barnes. 'Who's the lucky girl then, Victor?'

Victor's face turned scarlet. He stuffed the invitations back into his pocket and hurried away, explosions of laughter rending the air behind him. After such a humiliation he was

determined to ask nobody else in his class. But he would have to find some guests from somewhere. What on earth was he to do?

On his way home from school, Victor called in at the Ice-Cream Parlour for a cornet. He didn't often eat ice-cream, but today Victor felt he needed some solace, some little treat to cheer himself up.

There was a customer at the counter in front of him, buying a huge plastic box of ice-cream. It was that nice Miss Anstey from 'Breezieways', the Children's Home just outside town; the place where orphan children lived whilst waiting to be fostered or adopted.

'Strawberry flavour, please; enough for twenty,' Miss Anstey laughed. 'Special treat today. We've got two birthdays at once, so we're having a little party.'

The two words 'twenty' and 'party' echoed on in Victor's mind. It took him a while to grasp their significance, but when he did, he suddenly shot out of the shop without waiting for his cornet. Breathlessly he chased Miss Anstey along the road.

'Excuse me – I couldn't help overhearing. You're from "Breezieways", aren't you?'

'Yes, that's right!' Miss Anstey regarded Victor with surprise. She didn't know this boy. Was he a would-be recruit, drawn by the lure of pink ice-cream?

'Well, I wonder....' Victor drew a great handful of invitations from his school bag. 'Would your children from "Breezieways" like to come to a party at our house on the twentieth?'

'What – all of them?'

'Yes, please. I'd like that very much.' Victor handed over the fat bunch of twenty invitations.

'Well, this is a surprise! Do you know some of our children, then?'

Victor had to admit that he didn't, but was keen to make their acquaintance, boys and girls alike. In fact, he had been waiting ages for an opportunity like this. He looked so earnest that Miss Anstey concluded he was trying to do his good deed for the year. And why not? More fortunate children, with secure, happy families, ought to reach out to their less privileged cronies. Here was an extended hand of friendship which Miss Anstey had no right to ignore. With a beaming smile she accepted Victor's invitation.

'One card will do for us all, though.' She selected one invitation from the top of the pile and handed back the rest. 'I'm sure you'll need these for your personal friends.'

Reading Victor's address, she added: 'Are you sure you'll have room for us all?'

'Oh, yes. My dad said he wanted it to be a really big party. He said it would be the best the town had ever seen. Something really special.'

'Well now, that *is* nice! We shall all look forward to it very much indeed, er' – here she checked the name on the card – 'Victor. You thank your parents for their kindness. It isn't

every day our children are invited out like this.'

Victor felt a wonderful lifting of the spirits. All of a sudden he was doubly virtuous. Not only had he given pleasure to twenty other people (twenty-one if you counted Miss Anstey) but he had also done his duty honourably. Now he had his full quota of guests and need not worry about the party

any more. On the day, the 'Breezieways' lot would play with one another, and he could sit happily in a corner, reading. He walked jauntily away, no longer in need of a soothing cornet.

He might not have felt quite so carefree if he had realised that there were actually thirty-eight 'Breezieways' children, eighteen of them being away on a trip for the day. Miss Anstey had understood that all thirty-eight were included in the invitation.

3
Classmates

'Hey, Victor!' called Becky Ward as Victor arrived at school next morning. 'You never gave us those invitations to your party.'

Victor froze.

'I thought you weren't coming.'

'What made you think that? We never said

we weren't, did we, Alison?'

'We never refuse a party,' Alison Barnes agreed. 'And you've invited us now, so you can't go back on it.'

Victor did not know how to deal with this situation. His social experience was so limited that he could not tell if the girls were serious or not. Must his original invitation really stand? He thought desperately for a minute, then decided that another two guests were neither here nor there. In fact, his dad might be pleased to find him so popular. He drew the wad of invitations from his bag and reluctantly handed a couple over. He must throw the rest of them in the dustbin as soon as possible. Or better still, burn them!

'Thanks, Victor! I'm going to wear my new party frock. Wait till you see it!'

'And I'm going to borrow my mum's lipstick.'

'Who else is coming?'

'Nobody you know,' said Victor uneasily.

Becky looked startled.

'What do you mean, nobody we know? Haven't you asked Lucy and Yvonne and Shamira? We always go to the same parties.'

'And what about the boys? I'm not coming if there aren't any boys.'

'There *will* be some boys,' said Victor a fraction too hastily. 'You just won't know them, that's all.'

'Won't *know* them?'

'Haven't you asked the rest of the class? If anyone in the class has a party they always ask everybody else; you know that. It's only fair.'

'*You* always get asked, Victor Lovat. We can't help it if you never turn up,' grumbled Alison.

It was true that the nearest Victor had ever got so far to a party was his great-uncle Walter's funeral tea, an admittedly depressing affair, apart from the turkey-and-stuffing rolls.

'Huh! We thought you were coming out of your shell at last. Should've known better.'

'I'll bet he's too shy to ask them,' decided Becky. With a determined snatch she relieved Victor of the rest of the invitations which he had still been clutching in his hand.

'Don't worry, Victor; we'll give them out for you.'

'Here, wait a minute – !'

But it was already too late. Becky and Alison were racing across the playground shouting happily to their cronies and waving Victor's colourful invitations temptingly in the air. They were soon the centre of a jostling, excited crowd.

By morning break, Victor was the picture of misery. He did not know what to do. He had been carrying the whole nineteen remaining invitations, and if Becky and Alison gave all those out he could see he was heading for disaster. His one hope was that he was so unpopular that very few people would actually want to come to his party. Perhaps the girls would have most of the invitations left, in which case he would burn

them at once.

No such luck!

Becky pounced on Victor the minute the bell went.

'We've run out,' she explained. 'Not enough invitations to go round. Can you give us another seven?'

'EH?' Victor gaped idiotically.

'Another seven,' repeated Alison impatiently. 'For the rest of the class.' Turning to Becky she added: 'I do believe he's not bought enough to start with. Would you credit it?'

'Can't count! Never mind; he can nip in to Woolworth's on the way home and get some more. Bring them tomorrow morning, Victor and DON'T FORGET!'

'I – I've got no money.'

'Oh, honestly!' Becky cast her eyes up to the ceiling. 'Leave it to us, then. I've got some spares at home from my last party. I'll copy what it says on yours and give them out for you.'

'Well, actually…' Victor began, but Alison and Becky were already chasing off towards the biscuit-queue.

4
Cousins

When the sorely-troubled Victor reached home that afternoon, he wanted only to escape to his bedroom and lose himself in the latest 'Secret Seven' adventure, as far as possible from the grim reality of his complex and doom-laden life.

He opened the front door as quietly as he could, intending to creep across the hall and up the stairs without being spotted. But Mrs Lovat had been watching for her son, and the minute he came in she manoeuvred him into a quiet corner of the hall and whispered in his ear, casting wary glances over her shoulder in case her husband should overhear.

'Look, love, I know you're not keen on this party idea, and I daresay you'll be finding it hard to scrape together twenty guests. Your dad doesn't understand what it's like for a quiet, sensitive boy like you. Well, I don't want you to worry about it, because I've been able to help you out a bit. I've been round to your Auntie Ella's this afternoon and invited your cousins, James and Myra. I told them each to bring a friend as well. In fact, Myra's bringing two, as she says her best friends are twins.'

Mrs Lovat smiled proudly at her own initiative.

'So that's five guests already. Then I went

up to the vicarage with some jumble, so I mentioned it to the vicar and he said he would send his three children along as well. He was most sympathetic. He's a very understanding man, the vicar, and it didn't take him long to appreciate your problem. He was shy like you when he was a boy, he tells me, and he hated parties.'

By this time a trembling, white-faced Victor was holding on to the banister-rail for support, otherwise he would have tumbled in a shocked heap to the carpet. He tried to say something, but his throat produced only a croak. Mrs Lovat read these symptoms as sheer relief and patted his shoulder encouragingly.

'There now! I knew that would make you feel better. Your dad has no idea how much you worry about little things like this, but you know, he intends it all for the best.'

'M-Mum...' Victor at last managed to stammer.

'No; don't bother to thank me. As long as

you're happy, son, that's all that matters. Now, not another word; your dad might hear.'

Victor tried to climb the first step on his flight to oblivion, but it was too much for him. His legs would not seem to work properly. He remembered seeing a poster of an upward-gazing midget below a giant flight of steps, with the caption:

'This is what your stairs could look like to someone with heart disease.'

Well, that's exactly how Victor felt.

This party was going to be the death of him, just as he had realised from the first.

At that moment Victor's dad appeared.

'Well, how's it going, then?' demanded Arnold with a terrifying air of jollity.

Seeing that her son was stricken dumb, Mrs Lovat answered for him.

'He's got eight guests already,' she explained with pride.

'Is that all? Well, he'd better get a move on. It shouldn't be all that difficult, surely. In my day we were all raring to go to parties. You didn't have to ask us twice, I can tell you!'

Victor made a gigantic effort to pluck up his courage and confess. Clutching white-knuckled at the banister rail, he managed to whisper:

'Actually, Dad, there's been a bit of a mix-up.'

'Mix-up? You mean all your friends are going somewhere else that day? Well, why didn't you say so? We can change the date; no problem.'

'No, as a matter of fact, Dad, it's a bit more complicated than that.'

Victor might finally have made a clean breast of things, but again he was thwarted. The doorbell rang, and there on the doorstep were three of Mr Lovat's shipmates, come to bear him off to a darts match in a pub some miles away.

Mr Lovat was suddenly inspired.

'Here, I've just had an idea! If our Victor can only raise eight party guests we'll make up the number for him. Harry, George and Pete here can muster a kids' football team between them. Right, lads? Harry's got two girls and a boy; George has four sons, and Pete has two of each. What's more, seeing it's leave time, these three dads can come and help us with the games as well. I don't know why I never thought of it before.'

5
Gang

Next morning, Victor was late for school. He had never in his life been late before, but on this occasion he was desperate to avoid his classmates (who might even start asking for invitations for all their brothers and sisters) and had hidden himself under the railway arches for a solid twenty minutes, trying to decide what to do.

Could he ring up 'Breezieways' and tell them the party was cancelled? No, that would be a really rotten trick. Besides, the 'Breezieways' lot would probably declare war on him, and even if a few got killed in the process it would still only scrape the edge of the problem. The thing to do, he decided, was to make himself so detestable that nobody would want to come to his party after all. They would throw his invitations back in his face. Even Becky and Alison would cancel in disgust.

All right then, what did detestable people do?

After much desperate thought, Victor worked out a plan of campaign. First, he smeared mud on his face and clothes. (Mud was certainly something *he* detested.) Then he mussed up his tidy hair and undid his tie and shoelaces. Next, he practised a Frankenstein's Monster face, complete with extra squint, but this he abandoned as it made him feel dizzy. Finally he stamped through every filthy puddle he could find on his way to school, then burst rudely into the classroom instead of creeping meekly to his place as usual.

His teacher, Mrs Mason, opened her eyes very wide. When she demanded an explanation for Victor's lateness and unkempt appearance, he said cheekily:

'I had to take our goldfish to the vet. It's starting swimming sideways.'

Victor was amazed when the whole class guffawed appreciatively, and even Mrs Mason tried hard not to smile. She had worried about this timid boy for years. Now she was so delighted that Victor Lovat was showing signs of liveliness at last that her ticking-off was of the mildest kind.

This inspired Chris Wade to lean forward and deal Victor a congratulatory blow on the shoulder with his ruler. Normally, Victor would have borne this grievous bodily harm

with Christian fortitude but now, in his new detestable state, he turned round and punched Chris on the nose.

Although this skirmish miraculously seemed to escape Mrs Mason's attention, it was not lost on the rest of the class. Victor discovered that by break time, far from becoming detestable, his status had risen by several notches.

After more of the same behaviour in the second half of the morning, Barry Goodman actually invited Victor to join his gang!

The Goodman Gang!

The Under-Elevens Mafia, no less!

Victor had lived in terror of this gang throughout his school life. How could he possibly fraternise with *them*? He turned pale at the very thought.

'Me?' he enquired faintly.

'Sure!' Barry slapped Victor heartily in the ribs, knocking him halfway across the classroom. 'You've got all the right qualifications at last.'

'I have?'

It turned out that there were three conditions necessary to becoming a member of the Goodman Gang:

1. You had to look tough.
2. You had to punch somebody on the nose.
3. You had to think up a really daft excuse for a teacher and get away with it.

Did Victor really look tough? He glanced down at his bedraggled outfit and decided with amazement that today he probably did. He had certainly, by some incredible fluke, fulfilled the other two requirements. Perhaps he wasn't such a wimp as he'd always imagined? He straightened up a bit.

'Well,' he began more boldly, 'what exactly does this gang do?'

'Do? We practically run this school, for a start. And we stick up for one another. "All for one and one for all." '

'What else?'

'How does he mean, "what else?" ' Chris Wade cried indignantly.

'Look, just make your mind up, Lovat. Do you want to join, or don't you? You won't get asked again!'

''Course he wants to join!'

'Come on, Victor! We only need one more member, then we'll be the biggest gang in the district.'

'I don't know what you're dithering about for; we're doing you a favour. There are kids who would give their second front teeth to be in our gang.'

'So why don't you let them?' Victor could

not help thinking. 'Then you would be the biggest gang in the district.' Still and all, it was flattering to be wanted. Victor could easily have lost his head at this point and given in. But you don't abandon a whole way of life without deep consideration.

'I'll have to think it over,' he said.

'You *what*?'

'Who does he reckon he is?'

'Oh, leave him! He'd be no good to us anyway. Can you see a crumb like him solving members' problems?'

This was the point at which Victor really pricked his ears up. So the gang went in for problem-solving, did they? Well, that was a different matter. If anyone had a problem that needed solving, it was Victor Lovat.

'All right,' said Victor suddenly, 'you can count me in.'

'I should bloomin-well think so!'

'Good job for you!' said Barry Goodman darkly. 'Nobody turns us down and lives to tell the tale.' All the same, he felt he ought to make sure of Victor right away. 'Come round to the back of the boiler-house quick, and we'll swear you in.'

Victor was marched away like a human sacrifice. It was not a pleasant experience. Had he made the wrong decision after all? How complicated life could be! If only he hadn't been forced into having this wretched party, none of this would have happened and he could have got on with his peaceful, solitary, entirely satisfactory existence.

'Right, then!' Barry produced a fearsome-looking darning-needle from the lapel of his jacket.

'Here's what you do. Prick your thumb with this, Comrade Lovat. (Oh go on! A bit harder than that; don't be so soft!) Now make a bloody circle with a dot in it, right in the middle of your forehead. (A *circle* I said!) Now hold up your left hand, swear eternal secrecy and allegiance to your leader (that's me) and spit three times into this empty matchbox.'

Phew!

Was that it? Victor felt quite exhausted.

'Now all you have to do is repeat the gang's motto three times: "All for one and one for all." We do everything together, see? Everything! That means we need another five invitations to your party for a start, as some of our gang come from Cobb Street School.'

Oh no! Not more invitations!

But it was too late now; Victor was a sworn-in member of the gang.

His horror was short-lived, however, as he remembered the problem-solving which was to follow. After all, the bigger his problem, the more worthwhile it would be for the gang to solve it. In fact, the swearing-in had induced in Victor a mood of recklessness. If he could survive that, he could survive anything.

There was a gang meeting after school that day, in Barry Goodman's garage. Victor had never been late home before, and guessed his parents would not be too pleased, especially when they saw the state his clothes were in. But he had taken the plunge now, and his conscience seemed to be drowning in the deep end.

During the maths lesson Victor had managed to print out five more home-made party invitations which he now distributed to the gang's Cobb Street School contingent. Then he settled down impatiently to await the first problem-solving session.

It turned out that any member could bring along a problem to any meeting and the gang would work on it together. Today, for instance, one lad announced that he had been given the job of looking after his kid brother at the time of the next gang meeting, so several other members volunteered the services of their sisters, brothers or cousins as substitute baby-minders. There was such a good response that the lad was able to make a leisurely choice.

Another lad had accidentally broken a neighbour's window and needed a certain amount of financial help to repair the damage. There was a quick whip-round, each gang member contributing as much as he could afford. Victor handed over the change from his dinner-money, hoping that his mother would forget to ask for it.

After witnessing the neat disposal of several such problems, Victor asked eagerly: 'Can I tell my problem now?'

Barry Goodman gave him a bossy glare.

'Not at your first meeting. You'll have to wait until Friday.'

Victor's face fell. Friday wouldn't leave him much time.

'It's urgent!'

'Rules are rules. New members can't bring up a problem before their third meeting. You need to prove your loyalty first.'

'But you'll settle it on Friday, will you? It's quite a big problem.'

''Course we'll settle it! No problem's ever beaten this gang yet.'

Well, that was something to be thankful for. Victor turned his thoughts to the more immediate problem of being late home.

6
Full house

'You know,' worried Mrs Lovat, 'I'm beginning to think this party's had more effect on our Victor than you bargained for. Ever since you mentioned it I've been noticing changes in the boy.'

'About time, too!' retorted Mr Lovat from

behind his newspaper.

'He's getting a lot less reliable, for a start. Comes home at all hours. Takes no pride in his appearance any more. Even lost his dinner-money change.'

'He's livening up, that's what it is. Spends a lot less time with his nose in a book, and a good thing, too!'

'Oh, don't pretend you object to reading! I notice you've got your nose in a newspaper half the time.'

'He's making some friends at last, and that's what matters.'

'Yes, and what sort of friends? I saw him in the street the other day with some very rough-looking lads. It's just as well we chose the guests for his party, or he might have invited some of them. I wouldn't have fancied that.'

'You're too soft with him! How's he going to grow up into a man if you molly-coddle him all the time?'

Mrs Lovat was beginning to lose her

temper. 'I don't molly-coddle him! I let him be himself and do what he enjoys doing, instead of bullying him all the time like some I could mention. You know very well he doesn't like parties, and if you must know, I think it's cruel to make him have one.'

Mr Lovat threw down his newspaper with a violent gesture.

'Well, he's having one, and that's an end of it. If you ask me, it's a good job I came home when I did. A boy needs a dad around the place.'

'Oh, you think so, do you? Well, let me tell you....'

The argument was warming up considerably, and by the time Victor came home a great many unfortunate things had been said. Mr Lovat had seen a side of his wife's character that he had hitherto been quite unfamiliar with, and the atmosphere was as tense as a dentist's waiting-room.

But Mrs Lovat was not too angry to think of her son.

'Sssh!' she whispered hastily. 'Victor's home! Don't let him hear us quarrelling or he'll be really upset.'

Victor, however, had noticed nothing. He had enough problems of his own to worry about. He ran straight upstairs to practise his speech for tomorrow's meeting.

'You see, Comrades, it's like this. I've invited too many folks to my party and my parents will go scatty.'

No, no; that wouldn't do! Being guests themselves, the gang might take offence and think Victor's parents didn't want them. He'd have to be a bit more subtle. How about: 'We're having a little difficulty with space'? Oh, dear! It wasn't as easy as it seemed.

By the time Friday came, Victor was so anxious about his problem that he ran straight out of school the minute the bell went, and was first to arrive at Gang Headquarters. For a horrible moment he thought he'd got the day wrong, or that nobody was going to turn up, but one by one the members drifted in, and soon they were applying their joint ingenuity to Victor's dilemma.

'We could start an epidemic,' Chris Wade suggested. 'Hasn't your sister got chicken-pox, Dodger?'

She had; but Dodger didn't think his mother would let her out of bed to go breathing all over folks.

'No need. She could write germy letters. One to "Breezieways"; one to everybody in our class except us, and one to Victor's cousins.'

'Don't forget the vicarage and my dad's mates' kids,' put in Victor anxiously.

'How can she write to them when she doesn't even know them?' asked Dodger reasonably. 'Anyway, she's only five, so she can hardly write at all.'

'All right then, we could send threatening letters from the gang. "Stay away from Victor Lovat's party, or else…."'

Not many were in favour of that idea.

'It'd take more than that to scare *me* off a party.'

'Yeah, they'd all guess who'd written the letters anyway.'

'The "Breezieways" lot would gang up on us. Not that you could blame them.'

'And who's gonna pay for the stamps?'

There was a gloomy silence, then one of the Cobb Street bunch announced: 'There's a lad in our school who's absolutely hopeless at conjuring tricks, though he thinks he's the bee's knees. Gets every trick wrong all the time. We could ask him to do a turn at the party and that would put everybody off coming.'

'You mean Lenny Hargreaves? You're telling me he's hopeless!'

'Pathetic, more like!'

'I once saw him do a stunt called "The Vanishing Accomplice" and it was a complete fiasco. Talk about laugh!'

'He'd ruin any party, he would.'

'Right! That's it, then. He can ruin Victor's. Start a rumour that Hargreaves is going to do his stuff, and Bob's your uncle!' Barry was tired of Victor's problem, yet did not wish to lose face by finding no solution. This Lenny Hargreaves was obviously the answer, and the matter was now closed.

'Next item on the agenda!'

Victor was disgusted. After a whole session's thought, the only result had been to add yet another two guests – Lenny Hargreaves and his accomplice – to the party list, and Victor knew it wouldn't work anyway. He had seen Lenny Hargreaves's performance himself, and knew that he played to packed houses because everyone *wanted* to laugh and sneer at his mistakes. His act might even tempt a crowd of gate-crashers.

What a fiasco!

Victor took the short cut home across the graveyard, feeling so miserable by now that he almost hoped a ghost would rise up and frighten him to death. That would be one way out of his troubles. Failing that, it looked as though he would either have to run away or get himself turned into a frog. Anything to escape that great, howling mob throwing stones at his windows on party day when they found they couldn't even get into the house, let alone sink their teeth into his mother's chocolate cake.

'All for one and one for all' indeed!

Fat lot of good the gang had been to him. Why, they were no smarter than he was. He didn't know why he had been so scared of them all these years. He would cancel his membership on Monday – if he was still around by then.

At that moment a sinister shape material-ised from behind one of the larger tomb-stones and began advancing towards Victor through the rain. Victor stood absolutely still. Now that his half-wish had come true, he was suddenly scared to death.

The rain had made the sky so dark that

Victor felt anything could happen in this spooky place. His whole life ran fast-forward through his brain as he cowered against the plinth of a giant marble cross. Suppose there were soon another marble cross?

HERE LIES THE BODY OF

SCHOOLBOY VICTOR LOVAT

FRIGHTENED TO DEATH ON

FRIDAY THE THIRTEENTH…

Now, too late, he could see that his party problem was as nothing compared to the horrors of a tangle with the supernatural. In fact, it was such a puny, insignificant problem that he could not think why he had been so worried about it in the first place. He needed to get his priorities right. People were only people; nothing to be afraid of after all. If only the spectre spared him he'd go home and confess.

Victor stood trembling as the sinister shape continued to advance, until suddenly, with a great lurch of relief, he realised who it was.

'Dad!'

'Oh, there you are, son. I've been looking for you.'

It turned out that Mr Lovat was on his way to the vicarage to seek advice. This seemed strange to Victor, as Mr Lovat was not a religious man.

'What's up, Dad?'

Mr Lovat took a deep breath, and a hard, stubborn look came into his eye; a look with which Victor was not unfamiliar.

'This party of yours. Me and my mates were talking about it again, wondering how we could make it a really tip-top affair, not just your ordinary run-of-the-mill party, and we came up with a few great ideas.'

'What sort of great ideas?' Victor was already alarmed.

'The whole thing needs livening up. These tame little party games your mother's thought up are no good at all for lads like you. You need something with a bit more zing in it. We thought we could put on a cabaret, for a start. You know, hornpipe, sea-shanties and a funny sketch or two. George and Harry are especially good at the footwork and Pete's a born comedian.'

'But Dad – !'

'The only trouble is,' Mr Lovat went on, ignoring the interruption, 'there won't be enough room for all that at home, so we'll have to get the vicar to hire us the church hall. I was just on my way to fix it up. Of course, when we do that, twenty children are going to look a bit lost in that great big room, so we'll have to find a few more guests from somewhere. More than a few, in fact.'

There followed a moment's silence, during which Mr Lovat peered anxiously at his flabbergasted son. To tell the truth, Victor's dad felt more than a little guilty about these last-minute changes, which were the defiant result of the quarrel with his wife. (After all, he had to show who was boss.) He could not help remembering Mrs Lovat's prediction, though: 'This time you've gone too far. Much, much too far!'

He was just wondering whether to cancel the whole wretched party after all, when Victor came joyously to life. To Arnold's absolute astonishment, his son leapt nimbly away over the gravestones just like any normally boisterous boy, face beaming like a lighthouse through the rain.

For Victor's problem was solved!

There was no need for confession; all his invitations could stand.

Furthermore, there would now be so many guests at his party that his own presence there would hardly be noticed. As soon as he had welcomed everybody and shown his face, he could sneak off home and read his library book in peace.